Thomas William Hodgson Crosland

Literary Parables

Thomas William Hodgson Crosland

Literary Parables

ISBN/EAN: 9783744747455

Printed in Europe, USA, Canada, Australia, Japan

Cover: Foto ©Andreas Hilbeck / pixelio.de

More available books at **www.hansebooks.com**

LITERARY · PARABLES

BY · T · W · H · CROSLAND

LONDON · AT · THE · UNICORN
PRESS · A.D · MDCCCXCVIII

NOTE

*Nos. I. to XXXVI. and Nos. XXXVIII.,
XLIII., XLVI., LI., LIII., and LV.,
are reprinted, by kind permission, from THE
ACADEMY.*

4

Contents

I

The Dream

A starveling poet dreamed in his sleep that it was decreed that he might never put pen to paper again. And he felt rather sorry. And then he awoke and felt sorrier still.

II

Conditions

They thrust a lark into a prison of wires, and blotted out the blue above him; and he shook the spaces of the day with song.

Whereas a sparrow, blown by chance into the seventh heaven, might still do no more than chirp.

III

Classification

The morning stars sang together.
And a person of delicate ear and nice judgment discussed the singing at length, and showed how and wherein one star differed from another, and which was great and which was not.
And still the morning stars sang together.

IV

Suggestion

A man ranged cowslips on a stall, and wondered how many he should give for a penny.

And another man, passing, caught the gleam and the odour of them, and had a vision of a blue valley touched with gold, and April scattering desultory rains.

V

The Four Wishes

Four men of letters wished each a wish. The first one wished that he might never lack bread; the second, that he might compass great riches; and the third, that his name might endure indefinitely.

And the fourth and maddest of them wished for a gift to filter good things into style, without regard to bread, or gain, or fame.

VI

Justified

The stars accused the moon of plagiarism. And they sent word to the nightingale not to commend her, saying, " She deceiveth thee, and borroweth this beauty."

"Even so," answered the nightingale. "Yet which of you will tell me that she borroweth not to advantage ? "

VII

The Merely Marketable

A pollo told the Muses that a mediocre writer was making too much play with his pen, and compassing a great deal of supererogatory tarantara.

And the Muses retorted that it was scarcely their fault, inasmuch as not one of them had been near the man.

VIII

Moods

A young man sat in a rose-garden and wooed
Death with sonnets.

And later Death came to do him courtesy;
but he said, "Nay, nay, not yet! . . . I have
much to write."

14

IX

Fiction

A king, making a progress through his dominions, came suddenly on a glittering villa, the like of which, with its gables and turrets and palm-house and gorgeous front garden, he did not remember to have seen before.

And he inquired of his equerry to what person of rank and fortune such magnificence might belong.

"That, sir," answered the equerry, "is one of the residences of Mister Brilliant, the great story-writer."

"Bless my soul!" gasped the king.

X

The Acceptable

Unto the Mistress of great writing they brought their newest poet. And she said : " I wish him well."

And upon a succession of honest fictionists she smiled.

And one followed, who, to use his own word, " bought 'em all and read 'em all."

Then she looked splendid things.

Incorrigible

They set two men in the stocks—one, a tinker, who had rioted on small ales; the other, a ballad-maker, who, by vile diction, had offended the public taste.

And about noon the tinker broke silence, and observed, "Master Ballad-maker, these melancholy hours will not be wasted; for I have now devised means whereby, on our releasement, good store of liquor may be procured."

"And, for my part," responded the ballad-maker, "I rejoice to say that I am hit upon a most seductive collocation of rhymes!"

XII

Meetings

The sun and the moon had heard a great deal of each other.

And one afternoon they chanced to be in the firmament together.

"Washed out!" said the sun.

"Jaundiced!" said the moon.

XIII

"This Also—"

"When I have climbed unto exaltation," quoth Promise, "I look to make myself passably snug."

"Young man," remarked Performance, "victuals have no sweeter savour on the pinnacle than in the valley."

Done

Circumstance got a poet by the throat, and well-nigh squeezed the life out of him. And the poet begged, chokingly, for mercy.

"Will you write fiction, then?" demanded Circumstance.

"Yes," gasped the poet, "I suppose I must!"

So that he went and fashioned a plot, and set it round with his best; eschewing only rhyme and measure.

And forthwith Circumstance began to be very kind to him.

And the poet laughed in his sleeve.

XV

On the Shelf

"You really have no business here, you know," said the book of verse to the paper-backed novel.

"Oh—why not?"

"Well, to be frank, you are not literature."

"But I am in my sixty-sixth thousand!"

Out of Date

On a May morning a youth lay under a hedge and wept, and railed at Fate.

And by and by an ancient man came that way, and said to him, "You appear to be in sore trouble!"

"Alas," replied the youth, "my case is indeed sad: I am a neglected genius!"

"Dear, dear!" observed the ancient man. "Then surely you must be the last of them!"

Medium

A worker in verse made a book upon Love, and got nothing for it. And a worker in prose made a book upon the same matter, and was able to take his family to Bexhill for a week.

"It is a mundane world," said the verseman.

"But it suits *me* very well," said the proseman.

XVIII

The Eternal Book

Quoth the miller's wife to the miller : " An thou visit this fair, thou shalt buy us all a faring ; as, a top for Jack, ribands and a necklet of bugle for Marian, and combs for each of the maids."

" And for thyself ? "

" For myself, good lack, I desire a sweet love-tale stuffed with piteous words."

Réchauffé

A piper stood in the market-place and piped a tune so villainous that the people assailed him with blows.

And next year he came again with a new tune that set them all a-dancing.

And they filled his hat with ha'pence, and said, "Excellent!—now play something else!"

And being more or less put to it for matter, the piper ventured on the tune for which, a twelve-month back, he had suffered blows.

And the people were ravished.

XX

Criticism

The small birds told the owl that he must not say "This will never do" again. "For," they added, "we are agreed that it is your business to stimulate with praise; to search out ambushed beauty; and to interpret to the advantage of the interpreted."

"You conduct your affairs with singular acumen," remarked the owl.

The Seasonable Lyrist

"One can think of nothing more delightful."
"Than what?"
"Than to have to be continually standing tiptoe upon little hills for a living."

XXII

Success

A man of letters was accused of harbouring Success.

"It is true," quoth the culprit. "She came to my door in the night; I took her in; my wife was charmed with her; and we decided to let her stay. Also: we have not regretted it."

XXIII

The Other Party

A man called upon the gentle reader and offered him condolences on the ethereal mildness of criticism, the reckless over-production of books, and the hypothetical standards of value set up by authors and publishers.

And the gentle reader answered softly, that he was much obliged, but that these things really didn't concern him, because he read for pleasure only, and never read anything that was not supplied from the libraries.

XXIV

Proletary

"The people are entirely soulless," quoth a poet.

"Yet if you and I do not in some way touch them, we perish," quoth another.

30

XXV

Equipment

Said the mother to the fairy, "It is my desire that this babe should wax with years into an effective man of letters."

"Wherefore," answered the fairy, "I will give him the three things most necessary to such a man—namely, a nimble brain, a liberal heart, and a thick skin."

Foreword

A reviewer sat in his arbour with a parcel of small poets, trying to find reasons for saying something pleasant about each of them.

And by and by he lit upon a chaste, vellum-and-gilt duodecimo, on page 5 of which he read: "To THE CRITICS.—Be indulgent. I write my poems because they come; and they are now given to the world at the earnest solicitation of my friends. For the peck of faults in this book I blush; but haply some poor rhyme of mine may ease the aching heart of——"

"Wife!" roared the reviewer, "bring me my grievous crabtree cudgel!"

Altitude

They brought a mad poet before the king.

"Give us something fine, now," said the king.

"Faugh!" the poet exclaimed, "I have ceased to dabble with words!"

"He is not so very mad," remarked the king.

XXVIII

Reasonable

"This is, no doubt, an excellent work," quoth the publisher, "yet I am afraid the public would not buy it."

"I never suggested that they would," replied the author. "Indeed, if one may be candid, the thing was written for Posterity."

"That being the case," said the publisher, "why not get Posterity to produce it?"

The Personal Note

" Eheu ! " sighed a poet, " the people will *not* be moved; and I have shown them my heart ! "

" *Thy* heart," quoth his friend, " is nothing. . . . Show them *their own* ! "

XXX

Value

A burgess of the city of letters hied him to the mayor, with the complaint that the city musicians were only a very middling lot.

"Perhaps you are right," said the mayor, "but I think we get a pretty adequate return for the wages we pay them."

XXXI

Curious

In the spring he gave them poesy. And they said, "This man hath indubitable gifts. He rhymes well, thinks delicately, and knows his way to the profound emotions. And yet, and yet, and yet—he is not of the company!"

So that next autumn he hazarded a volume of prose. And they said, "Now here we have a true poet!"

XXXII

Wisdom

A man met a publisher on the top of a mountain. "Hello!" said the man, "what are you doing here?"

"Looking for new talent," answered the publisher.

"You are too high up," observed the man. "Better go down to the middle slope, and discriminate."

But the publisher said he thought he should remain where he was.

XXXIII

Mercantile

He inquired of an old wise man whether it were sinful to write for money.

And the old wise man answered, " There be two kinds of writers, my son : to wit, those who write for money and get it, and those who write for money and *don't* get it."

XXXIV

The Benign Mother

"Poverty never did any good in the world," cried the reformer.

"Yet she appears to have stood in a maternal relation to considerable fine writing," observed the philosopher.

XXXV

The Untameable

Fate forgot to clip a poet's wings. So that there was no holding him, and his friends despaired.

And then a book he had written began to sell. And within the lapsing of a moon you might have seen him eat sugar out of ladies' hands.

XXXVI

Mobbed

A popular writer complained that it was impossible for him to go abroad without being followed and stared upon by gaping vulgarity.

" You shouldn't have had so many photographs taken," remarked his friend.

XXXVII

The Potboiler

The people read his book, and laughed and wept at the appointed places, and said it was "great," and ran about recommending it to their friends.

And for all that he wished it unwritten.

XXXVIII

The Single Art

A swan who dwelt on the bosom of a mere was vastly admired by a fox, who one day said to her, "How gracefully you swim! Now, though envious people tell me otherwise, I make no doubt that you would cut an equally elegant figure on the grass here."

Pleased with this flattery, the swan came ashore and essayed to walk; but waddled so, that the fox laughed consumedly.

"Ah, madam," quoth he, "I am afraid it is given to few of us to do more than one thing really well."

XXXIX

Heredity

Her lips were like a thread of scarlet. And he saw her, and had a mind to marry her, and said so.

"Alas, I do not know you, sir!" pouted she.

"Really? Well, my name is Romeo, and I have a comfortable publishing business, and——"

But she screamed and fled, for she was the daughter of a maker of ballads.

XL

The Fashion

A prince determined to take to authorship. And he called for his fool and told him of his purpose, adding that he thought he should begin by producing a considerable poem.

"Well," remarked the fool, "if you do it in the best modern minor manner, it is simply a question of saying nothing, finely."

XLI

Brethren

A tinker read a sweet poem about the brotherhood of man.

And later he spied the author of that poem in the market-place, and ran up to him, and grabbed him by the hand, and said, "My brother—my dear brother, let us go and pick a bit o' dinner together!"

And the poet answered that he was not in the habit of picking bits of dinner with persons whom he did not have the honour to know.

XLII

Silenced

" I   must sing the new song," said a poet.
    "Then get thee down into the cities, and hearken."

And the poet went into the cities.

And on a night he returned.   " I have heard it," he said . . . "and I shall sing no more."

Equation

Two men of letters met in the workhouse.

"My friend," cried one of them, "what evil brought you to this?"

"Sloth!" replied the other. "And *you*—how came *you* here?"

"Alas, sir! Have you forgotten that I am a stylist?"

7 49

XLIV

The New Poet

The new poet sat on a green hill.

And they brought him tidings of the death of the king's cousin.

"Quite so," quoth the poet. "Here is a threnody."

"Also," said they, "a princess hath been happily delivered of a male child."

"I shall felicitate her Highness in sweet verses," said the poet.

"And," they continued, "it is now the time of the year for the putting forward of rhythmical trifles wherefrom the delicate few may derive delectation."

"There is a bundle of such trifles," the poet answered.

"And the people, the common people, that dwell in the shadows and are eaten up of penury and squalor and the cupidity of the mighty; it were meet that thou had'st some word for *them*."

"Ah," mused the poet, . . . "the dear people!
. . . I have nothing for the people!"

XLV

At the Bottom of the Well

A man married a fair woman and had great joy of her for a year ; when it chanced that he suffered reverses, and had not much money.

And being brought unto meagre chiffons and serviceable hats, the fair woman grew surly and cold, and at length broke out into reproaches, and packed her boxes, and would go home to her mother.

Then the man said to her, " My child, I am astonished ; for though Adversity is a taxing housemate, yet hath she ever lent a peculiar tenderness to wifely love ; and this you may read in all the books."

" Fiddle-de-de ! " snapped the fair woman, " the sooner you learn that the facts of life are not published at six shillings, the better will be your chances of attaining wisdom."

XLVI

Shocking

"Go carefully with young So-and-so."
"Ah, why?"

"He brought me his first story: and as it was pretty good, I told him that we might deal. And then he asked me what sum I intended to pay him on account of royalties."

"Dear, dear, dear, dear, dear, dear, dear!"

XLVII

Reading

"Have you read the law?" asked the priest. "Through and through," replied the poet.

"Then pray recite to me some passage therefrom."

"Nay! That, I am afraid, is beyond me."

"Truly," said the priest, "you are a pretty reader."

"Sir," responded the poet, "if I may make so bold, have you bathed to-day?"

"I am just come from the pools."

"Then please give me a few drops of water."

"Tush!" answered the priest, "I bathe not that I may carry away water, but for the health and refreshment of my body."

"And I read," remarked the other, "not that I may accumulate phrases, but for the health and refreshment of my spirit."

XLVIII

Taste

"I say," cried the duchess's parrot to the thrush, "do please stop that row!"

But the thrush sang on.

And coming forth to take the sun, the duchess remarked to one of her women, "What a brave melody that thrush gives us!"

"Delightful, delightful, delightful!" bawled the parrot.

Scansion

A poet made a poem that took the breath.
And the clever writers marvelled.

And one of them went and read all about prosody, and said, "Thank God! This is a pretty good poem, but there are quite three lines in it which we prosodists may not scan!"

L

Cut

A sapling in the king's orchard complained that he had been cruelly hurt by the pruner.

"It is a shameful thing," he cried; "all my fairest branches are taken from me, and my wounds are many and grievous!"

"Hush," said an old tree, who overheard him, "and be of good heart, for nothing can happen to thee in this garden that is not for thy improvement."

Wanted

A man waited upon the secretary of the Department of Literature and asked for employment.

" What are you ? " inquired the secretary.

" Well, I have had extensive experience in the larding of reputations," quoth the man.

" Ah," sighed the secretary, " we are already very much overstaffed in that direction. What we need just now is a competent person to comb fools."

LII

Subsistence

" My voice is very beautiful," said the young thrush, "so beautiful, indeed, that I really don't see why I should have to hunt round for grubs like a common crow."

"If you look at things in that way," remarked his mother, "you had better go and get caught. It is the caged bird that sings for a livelihood."

Kindness

A budding poet brought an editor to task for not noticing his book.

Quoth the editor: "Sir, the verses were so foolish that it would have been impossible for me justly to praise them, and I had mercy."

"Knave!" cried the man of rhyme, "knowest thou not that I had rather be flayed alive than perish reviewless?"

Achievement

Two men climbed into a high tower to see the country.

One of them, a facile man, went up at a great pace; while the other, being slow of habit, scaled the stair with difficulty.

But both saw the country.

Short Measure

A Bodley poet died, and passed unto the country which hath been for the souls of poets from the beginning.

And while he was yet newly arrived, a company of souls waited upon him with a greeting, and inquired if he would be kind enough to inform them how he chanced to fare thither.

And he smiled and said, " I am the author of certain slight verses."

" What name ? " demanded they.

And he told them his name.

" We have heard of you," they answered. " Sixty-four heavy leaded pages triennally ! Now, everybody here hath written *tomes*—few or many, according to the number of his mortal years."

" Ay," remarked the Bodley poet, " and everybody in the world of the flesh is saying how badly all you fellows want editing down."

www.ingramcontent.com/pod-product-compliance
Lightning Source LLC
Chambersburg PA
CBHW022156020726
47496CB00008B/2751